For Noah, Anna, Dara, and Lincoln,
best monsterkids that I adore.

— AH

Published by Yeehoo Press
721 W Whittier Blvd #O, La Habra, CA 90631
www.yeehoopress.com

The illustrations for this book were created in watercolor, acrylics, crayons, pencil,
and mixed media as well as photography and photoshop.
This book was edited by Brian Saliba and designed by Xuyang Liu.

Library of Congress Control Number: 2020945558
ISBNs: 978-1-953458-01-8 (hardcover)   978-1-953458-02-5 (ebook)
Printed in China   First Edition
1 2 3 4 5 6 7 8 9 10

MY
MONSTERPIECE

AMALIA HOFFMAN

YEEHOO PRESS

I want to make the scariest monster ever!
It's going to have a long, green tongue.

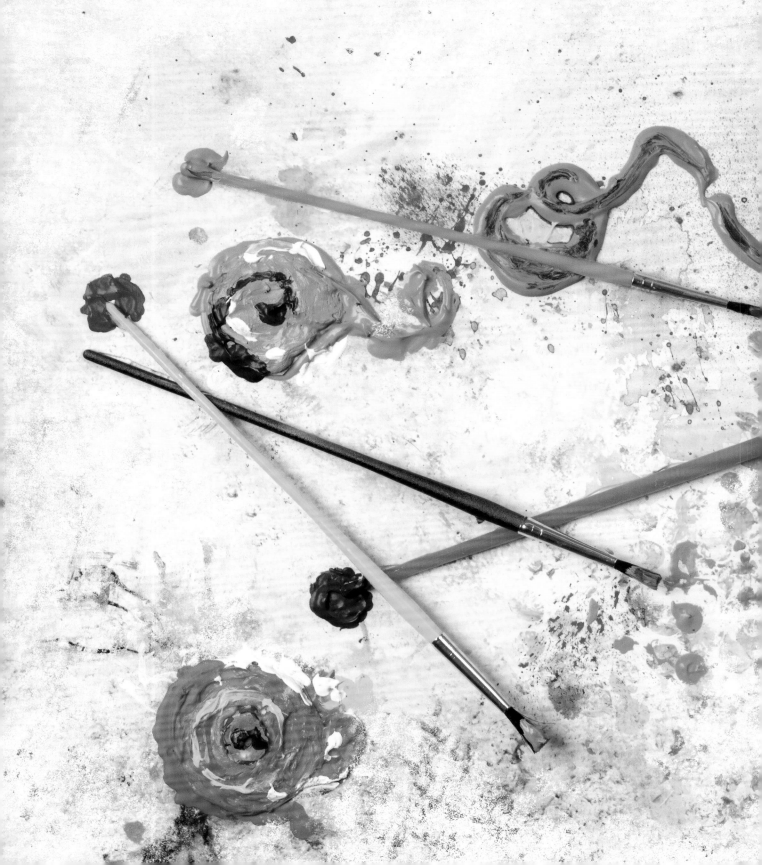

It will be a monster masterpiece —
MY MONSTERPIECE !

I sneak up on Mom,
who's munching on a chocolate chip cookie, and ...

"I love this chubby kitty,"
Mom says.

GRRRRR...

I guess my monster with the long, green tongue isn't scary.

What if I make a monster
with pointy horns on its head?

I sneak up on Dad, who's gobbling popcorn, and ...

RAHHHHHHH

"Great job painting an owl!"
says Dad. "May I hang it in my office?"

GRRRRR...

I guess my monster with pointy horns on its head isn't scary.

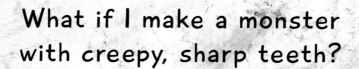

What if I make a monster
with creepy, sharp teeth?

I sneak up on my sister Sue,
who's coloring with crayons, and ...

Sue draws purple wings
on my monster.

"It's so cute!" she says.
"Is it the tooth fairy?"

GRRRRR

I guess my monster with creepy,
sharp teeth isn't scary.

So I make a monster with
a long, green tongue;
pointy horns;
creepy, sharp teeth;
and terrible claws too.

I sneak up on my best friend Jon,
who's building a sandcastle, and ...

RAHHHHH

"That's so funny!" Jon laughs.
"A tiger with chicken feet!"

I give up! I can't make a Monsterpiece.
My monsters aren't scary at all.

BUT WAIT,

I have an idea ...

Maybe monsters don't have to be scary!

What if there's a monster who loves
chocolate chip cookies, just like Mom?

What if there's a monster who
gobbles up popcorn, just like Dad?

What if there's a monster
who loves to color with crayons,
just like my sister Sue?

What if there's a monster
who loves building sandcastles,
just like my best friend Jon?

What if there's a monster who loves to make scary things, just like I do?

Would a monster like
that make pictures of
a scary kid?

Would he sneak up on his mom,
dad, sister, and best friend and ...

RAHHHHHHHHHHHH

What if his mom loves it?
And his dad asks to hang it in his office?
And his sister draws wings on it?
And his best friend laughs?

Maybe the monster would think ...

What if kids
don't have to be scary?

What if kids are ...

... JUST AS FUN AS MONSTERS.

TA DA!
MY MONSTERPIECE!